DONKEYS

Adelheid Dahimène-Heide Stöllinger
Translated by Catherine Chidgey

Edited by Penelope Todd

Jenny and Jack were planning their silver wedding anniversary. The two old donkeys had spent half their lives together, horsing around. When they first met they brayed, "HEE - HAW!" at exactly the same time. Snap! They got married on the spot.

They played
their favourite
donkey trick
every time
they crossed
a street.
Halfway
over they'd
dig in their
hooves
so hard
that nothing
in the world
could
budge them.

To help
forgetful
Jack
remember
their
wedding
anniversary,
Jenny
folded
down
the corner
of his ear
the night
before.

But what happened? The ear was blocked, and because he was already deaf in the other one, the rooster didn't wake him next morning. Jack slept through the clock striking twelve. He slept until nightfall. Jenny was furious. She gave a terrible snort. Jack had snored away the whole special day.

The donkeys yelled at each other:

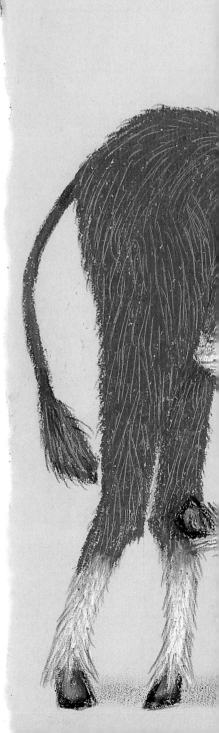

"SCREE-HAW!" "SCREE-HAW!" until Jenny turned on her heels and said, "I'm leaving!"

Now the pair had lived together so long it showed on their bodies. Jenny had a hollow on her neck from their countless hugs, while Jack had a bump in the very same place. They were a perfect fit.

Jenny bristled and hissed through her teeth, "There are plenty of other fish in the sea!"

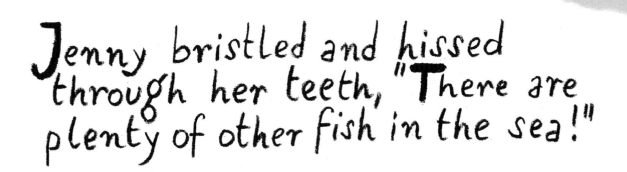

And off they trotted to find themselves a better match.

Jenny headed South
and Jack headed...South!

In a paddock Jack came upon a spotted cow.
Perhaps they'd make a good pair.
"How do you moo?" said the cow, staring
at his bump.

Jack stared back. The cow's hollow was patched with brown. He shuddered. **"SHE-HAWFUL!"**

Jenny met a billy-goat, but he only came up to her knees, which he tickled with his beard. **R**idiculous! she said to herself.

He was so scrawny and small, she'd never want to act the goat with him. Jenny left him and his bleating behind.

The donkeys went on searching doggedly. They chewed on the odd thistle to keep them going. Ever-hopeful, they fondled flamingos and huggled with hippos.

Trying to match up with a zebra, they began to see how pig-headed they'd been.

Would they ever find such a perfect match as that other old donkey?

Now the desert
stretched ahead.
Caravans of
camels snaked
through the dunes.
Jack saw their
lovely humps
swinging against
the sky.
He galloped
to meet them.

When night fell the camels lay down and tucked in together two by two. They looked like giant crabs in the sand. But there was one camel left over...

He gazed sadly at
the dunes stretching
their lonely humps into
the night. Jack crept up.
Jenny crept up too.

The camel pouted. "You make such a good pair. Don't you want to sleep now?"

Jack harrumphed, "**HEE-YEW!**" Jenny dug in her heels and stuck out her tail. "I've got nobody," said the camel. "I'll have to lie down in the dunes."

Jenny looked from the corner of her eye at the bump on Jack's neck. Through his thick lashes Jack saw that no one had taken his favourite hollow. They tested to see if they still fitted together. "You've lost weight," said Jenny. "Nonsense," said Jack. "Never mind," she said. "I'll have more room to breathe."

They sank down beside the sleeping camels. Between their donkey bodies there was just a chink of sorrow from their time apart.

The lone camel, however, came and lay upside down on the sand, his legs reaching into the desert sky — as a signpost for donkeys who lose their way.

First published in Austria
under the title ESEL
© 2002 by
Niederösterreichisches Pressehaus
Druck- und Verlagsgesellschaft mbH,
NP BUCHVERLAG
St. Pölten - Wien - Linz
www.np-buch.at

Reprinted 2005

English language edition
© 2005 by Gecko Press Ltd.

Published by Gecko Press Ltd, 11 Wright St,
Mt Cook, Wellington, New Zealand
www.geckopress.co.nz
Printed in China

GECKO PRESS